Little Seal

BENEDICT BLATHWAYT

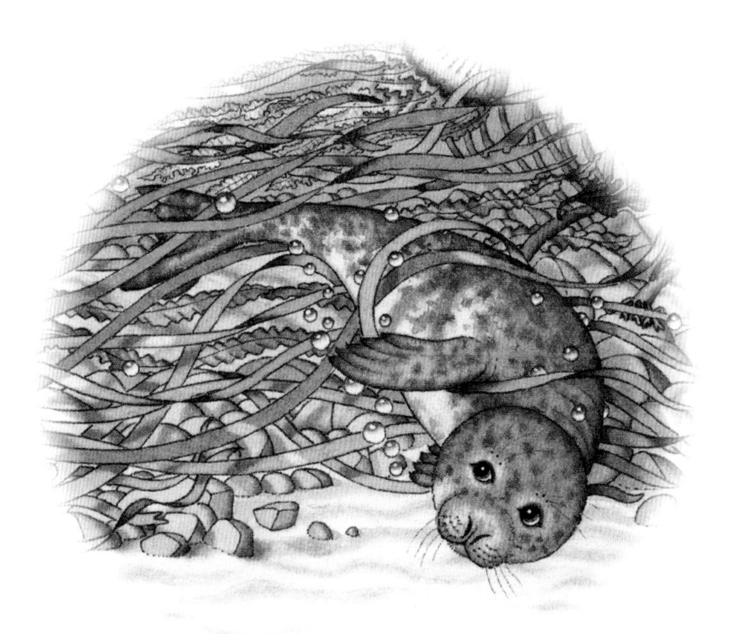

For Bessie

First published in 2017 by
BC Books
an imprint of
Birlinn Limited
West Newington House
10 Newington Road
Edinburgh EH9 1QS

www.bcbooksforkids.co.uk

ISBN: 978 1 78027 460 7

British Library Cataloguing-in-Publication Data
A catalogue record for this book is available from the British Library

Designed by Mark Blackadder

Printed and bound by Latimer Trend Ltd, Plymouth

Little Seal lived with his mother on a wild and lonely island.

He never went far from the beach where he had been born.

Little Seal grew up quickly, and his soft white coat turned a beautiful grey.

'Now you can go and play with the other young seals,' said his mother, 'and the whole of the huge, wide sea will be your home.'

But one night there was a terrible storm.

Little Seal was swept from the beach and
away from all the other seals.

'Whoo-oo-oo!' he cried out.

But there was no answer from the other seals; only the roar of the wind and the waves.

The tides and currents carried
Little Seal a long, long way from home.

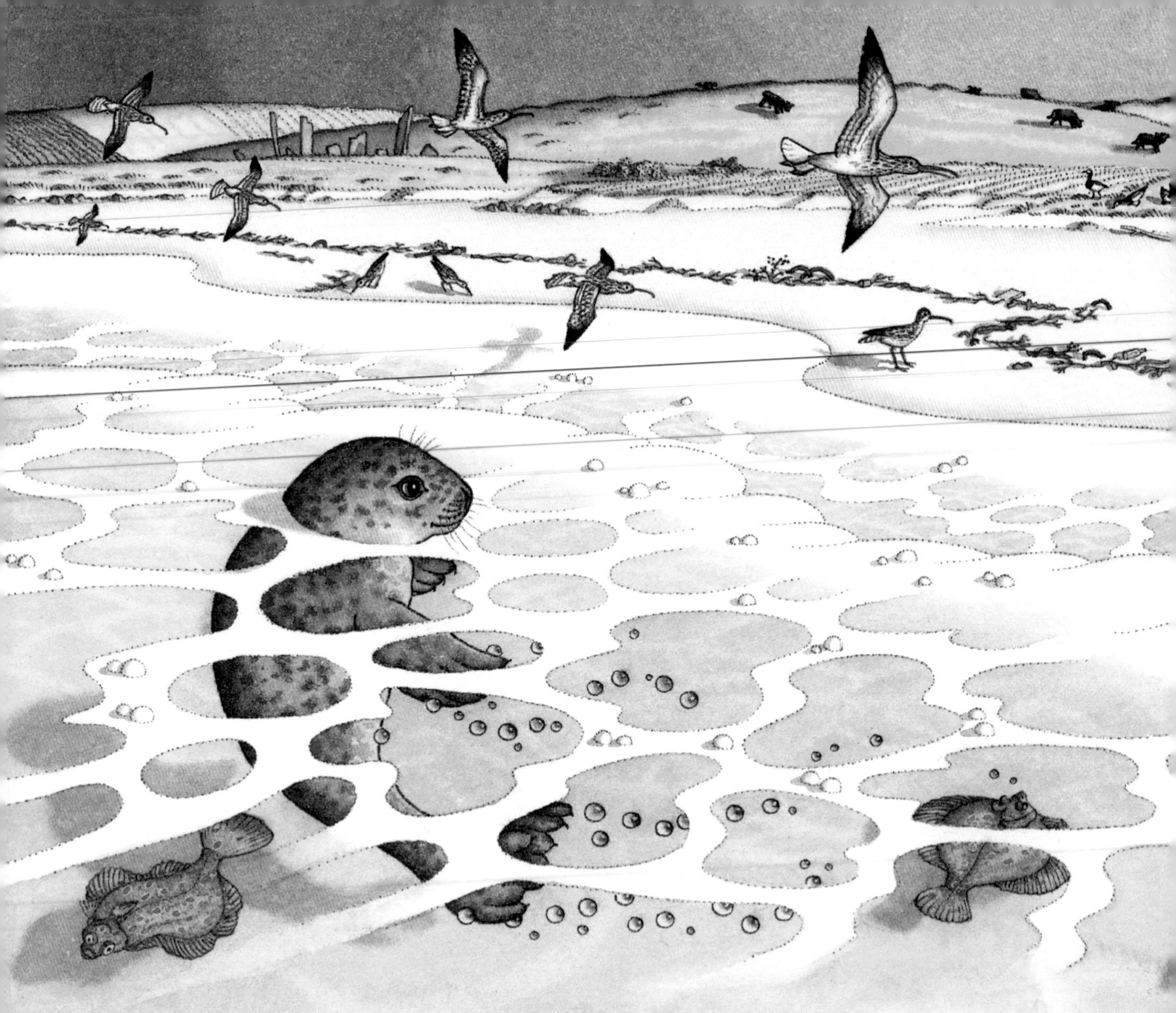

But in the morning, Little Seal was sure he could hear the other seals.
Was that them?

No, it was children playing with their dog on the sand.

And what strange noise was this?
Was it the other seals?

No, it was cows and sheep in the fields above the shore.

And in the harbour of the little town,
he thought he could hear the other seals.
But no, it was the crying of gulls overhead.

And what was the sound he could hear now?
Perhaps that was the calling of seals?

No, it was the hum of a ferry steaming by.

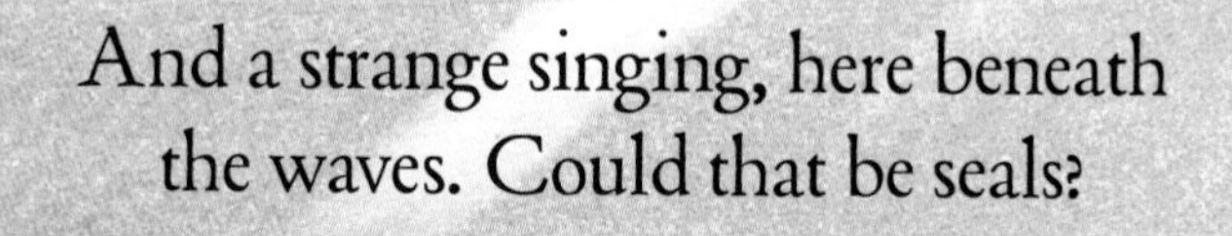

And a strange singing, here beneath
the waves. Could that be seals?

No, it was the deep, lonely song of a great big whale.

When night fell, Little Seal could hear nothing at all.

I do not like the huge, wide sea, thought
Little Seal, and it does not feel like home.

So he turned around and swam
back the way he had come.

How huge the waves were; how wide the sea!

And then Little Seal thought he could hear something.

It was not the sound of children or dogs or cows or sheep
or gulls or ferries or the lonely song of a great big whale ...

It was a voice just like his own: 'Whoo-oo-oo . . .'